NS

First published in Great Britain in 2003 by Andersen Press Ltd., 20 Vauxhall Bridge Road, London SW1V 2SA.
Published in Australia by Random House Australia Pty., 20 Alfred Street, Milsons Point, Sydney, NSW 2061.
All rights reserved. Colour separated in Switzerland by Photolitho AG, Zürich.
Printed and bound in Italy by Grafiche AZ, Verona.

10   9   8   7   6   5   4   3   2

British Library Cataloguing in Publication Data available.

ISBN 1 84270 220 3

I hate School

Jeanne Willis / Tony Ross

Andersen Press
London

This book has been printed on acid-free paper and is typeset in Century Schoolbook (of course!)

There was a fine young lady
And her name was Honor Brown,
She didn't want to go to school,
She hoped it would burn down.

And when I asked the child why,
Her little face turned red.
She threw her school hat on the floor
And this is what she said:

"My teacher is a warty toad!
My classroom is a hole!

The dinner ladies feed us worms,

And rabbit-poo and coal!"

And I believed her, every word –
For why should Honor lie?
And cling to mother on the step,

And stamp her feet and cry?

Weren't the lessons lots of fun?
And had she learnt to read?

"Oh, no," she said, "we don't do that,
They beat us till we bleed!

They throw us out of windows
And they make us walk on glass,

They always cut your head off
If you're talking in the class."

No wonder that she made a fuss
And didn't want to go –
But surely she had lovely friends?
Young Honor Brown cried, "No!

My friends are crooks and villains,
They are pirates! They are bad!

They are scary, spooky creatures,
They are monsters! They are mad!

They tied me to a rocket
And they sent me into space . . ."

No wonder little Honor Brown
Had such a grumpy face!

But what about the sandpit,
And the nice blue water tray?

"It would be fun," she said,
"If I could ever get to play.

The sandpit is a smelly swamp,
We sit in it and sink!

The water tray has sharks in,
They are killer sharks I think."

"Thank heavens for P.E.," I said,
"You love to swing on rope."
"Not by my neck I don't!" she said,
"Until I'm dead, they hope!"

"You liked the school trip, surely?
You had such a happy time."

She said, "I never did you know,
The coach was full of slime.

A tiger ate our teacher,
And it dragged her to its hut,

But far, far, far, FAR worse than that –

The ice cream shop was shut!"

Poor Honor Brown, poor little lamb!
They made her go each day,
The first year was the worst, she said,
She didn't want to stay.

The teacher stood her on the roof
Out in the snow and rain,
And when she fell off frozen stiff,
She sent her up again!

Her second year was dreadful . . .

On her Sports Day afternoon,
A wicked witch pushed past her
And her egg fell off its spoon.

Last summer term, a monster came
And scribbled on her work,

And no one would believe her –
The headmaster went berserk.

Yes, Honor Brown just hated school
For years and years and years,
Yet on the day that she could leave
I found her full of tears.

"Whatever's wrong?" I asked her,
"You no longer have to go."
But Honor Brown just howled, and sobbed . . .

"I'll really miss it though!"